THIS
GRAPHIC NOVEL
BELONGS TO:

_____

_____

PAPERCUTZ

#4 TRAPPED IN THE TRIASSIC

© 2019 KADOKAWA GEMPAK STARZ
All rights reserved.
Original Chinese edition published in Malaysia in 2011
by KADOKAWA GEMPAK STARZ SDN. BHD., Malaysia.
www.gempakstarz.com

All other Editorial material © 2019 by Papercutz.
All rights reserved.

REDCODE and ALBBIE—Story
AIR TEAM—Comics
REDCODE & SAMU—Cover Illustration
MAX—Cover Color
EVA, MAX, FUN, SENG HUI —Color
KENNY CHUA and KIAONG—Art Direction
ROUSANG—Original Design
BALICAT & MVCTAR AVRELIVS—Translation
ROSS BAUER—Original Editor
KARR ANTUNES —Editorial Intern
JEFF WHITMAN—Assistant Managing Editor
JIM SALICRUP
Editor-in-Chief

ISBN HC: 978-1-5458-0205-2
ISBN PB: 978-1-5458-0204-5

Printed in Korea
November 2018

Papercutz books may be purchased for business or promotional use.
For information on bulk purchase please contact Macmillan
Corporate and Premium Sales Department at (800) 221-7945 x5442

Distributed by Macmillan.
First Papercutz Printing.

DINOSAUR EXPLORERS Reading Guide
and Lesson Planner available at:
http://papercutz.com/educator-resources-papercutz

#4 TRAPPED IN THE TRIASSIC

REDCODE & ALBBIE – WRITERS

AIR TEAM – ART

PAPERCUTZ

NEW YORK

FOREWORD

Our planet is more than 4.5 billion years old, but we have only been around for 2 million! What strange creatures inhabited the Earth before we did?

While the DINOSAUR EXPLORERS series does refer to dinosaurs, the first two books focus on where the dinosaurs came from— and the creatures that even dinosaurs would call prehistoric! This series contains just as much fun as it does scientific information. Here you will see how our planet was transformed from a dry, barren ball of space rock into the haven it is today. You'll also see how the Earth's surface and seas formed, how single-celled microorganisms became complex multi-celled creatures, how bones evolved, and how we are not descended from monkeys, but fish!

Oh, yes, dinosaurs are the stars of the series, no doubt—from the magnificent Pterosaurus, to the fearsome Tyrannosaurus rex, to the Plesiosaurus and Ichthyosaurus, all mighty beasts of fact and legend. But even they had to start somewhere, and that is what we are going to discover!

And once we are done with dinosaurs and their beginnings, we can find out what happened and what life forms were around after the dinosaurs. We will take a look at the Cenozoic era, with creatures such as the Icarus bat, the sabre-toothed cat, and the woolly mammoth.
With great stories and science that will wow your friends and teachers, this DINOSAUR EXPLORERS graphic novel series from Papercutz is something not to be missed.

How the Earth was Formed

We know the Earth is the third planet in the solar system, the densest planet and, so far, the only one capable of supporting life. But how did that happen?

2 Formation of the Earth

As the Earth formed, its gravity grew stronger. Heavier molecules and atoms fell inward to the Earth's core, while lighter elements formed around it. The massive pressures from the external material heated up the Earth's interior to the point where it was all liquid (except for the core, which was under so much pressure it could not liquify). These settled down into the Earth's 3 layers: the crust, mantle, and core.

While we cannot say for sure just when these dust clouds solidified to form the Earth, nor when they came into being in the first place, we can tell that they took place more than 4.5 billion years ago.

1 The Sun's formation

Way, way back, there was a patch of space filled with cosmic dust and gases. Slowly, gravity (and a few nearby exploding stars) forced some of this dust and gases together into clumps–the gases formed into a massive, pressurized ball of heat which became the Sun, while the dust settled into planets, the Earth being one of them.

6 The Earth today

Even now, our Earth changes with time; its tectonic plates still move about on the lava bed of the mantle, pushing and pulling continents in all directions.

3 The crust

The crust was created around 4 billion years ago, as cooled, solid rock floating on the molten lithosphere merged. Even today, as the continental plates shift away and against each other, some of this rock and molten material might still change place.

4 The formation of the atmosphere

After our crust solidified, volcanic gases formed our atmosphere. The cooling surface allowed the formation of water vapor and bodies of water.

5 Land forms

Around 3.5 billion years ago, several land masses rose above the global ocean, giving rise to the continents we know today.

Geological Time Spiral

GEOLOGIC TIME SCALE

Evolution of Major Life-Forms

Years Ago

Cenozoic			Present
Quaternary	Holocene	Human era · Modern Plants	10 thousand
	Pleistocene		2.4 million
Tertiary	Pliocene		5.3 million
	Miocene		23 million
	Oligocene	Mammals	36.5 million
	Eocene		53 million
	Paleocene	Angiosperms	
Mesozoic			65 million
Cretaceous	Late Middle Early		135 million
Jurassic	Late Middle Early	Reptiles	205 million
Triassic	Late Middle Early	Gymnosperms	
Paleozoic			250 million
Permian	Late Middle Early		290 million
Carboniferous	Late Middle Early	Amphibians	355 million
Devonian	Late Middle Early	Pteridophytes	410 million
Silurian	Late Middle Early	Fishes	438 million
Ordovician	Late Middle Early	Psilopsida	510 million
Cambrian	Late Middle Early	Invertebrates	570 million
Proterozoic			800 million
Sinian			2.5 billion
Archaeozoic		Primitive single-celled creatures	4 billion

Phanerozoic

Proterozoic

Archaean

Cast

Sean (Age 13)
- Smart, calm, and a good analyst.
- Very articulate, but under-performs on rare occasions.
- Uses scientific knowledge and theory in thought and speech.

Stone (Age 15)
- Has tremendous strength, appetite, and size.
- A boy of few words but honest and reliable.
- An expert in repairs and maintenance.

STARZ
- A tiny robot invented by the doctor, nicknamed Lil S.
- Multifunctional; able to scan, analyze, record, take images, communicate, and more.
- Able to change its form and appearance. It is a mobile supercomputer that can store huge amounts of information.

Rain (Age 13)
- Curious, plays to win, penny wise but pound foolish.
- Brave, persevering, never gives up.
- Individualistic and loves to play the hero.

Dr. Da Vinci (Age 60)
- A professor at the National Scientific Research Institute.
- A genius inventor.
- Highly knowledgeable, loves adventure, but lazy by nature.

Diana (Age 30)
- Research-based Administrator, the Doctor's helpful assistant.
- A mature, beautiful, and capable lady.
- Good at problem solving.

Emily (Age 13)
- Smart, responsible, and adaptive.
- Calm under pressure, slightly vain.
- Computer savvy.

Particle Transmitter
- One of Dr. Da Vinci's most important inventions.
- Able to teleport the team to any period of time and space to execute their missions.
- Able to send urgently needed items to the team at any time.

PREVIOUSLY...

A massive earthquake sent the DINOSAUR EXPLORERS millions of years into the past, and when they first emerged in the Cambrian, they had no idea what to do! Though they managed to jump away in time (literally!) to avoid sinister Silurian sea life, they found that their Particle Transmitter only allowed them to travel several million years at a time—a problem when you are over 500 million years in the past!

Cambrian

Ordovician

Silurian

This came to a head in the Silurian when their worries and despair drove them to fighting among themselves. Incensed by Rain's jibes, Emily decided to set out with the DINOSAUR EXPLORERS to prove herself—and prove herself she did, facing everything from giant squid to sand-burrowing sea scorpions with guts and gusto!

Our heroes, heroines, and Dr. Da Vinci managed to escape the Silurian, only to end up facing the Devonian's major maulers, the Ichthyostega and Placodermi! Only a large dose of luck and dried fish saw them make their escape!

Things got bad in the Carboniferous when our protagonists and Dr. Da Vinci nearly became "Happy Meals" for some super-sized bugs! Giant spiders, giant dragonflies, and giant frogs (they might not have been bugs, but they were BIG!) all stood in the way of their attempt to study and escape the Carboniferous!

| Devonian |
| Carboniferous |
| Permian |
| Triassic |
| Jurassic |
| Cretaceous |
| Tertiary |
| Quaternary |

They then found themselves in the Permian, stuck with the proto-reptiles whose species would evolve into dinosaurs! Things only got more complicated when the Explorers discovered that their latest assignment included dino babysitting. Though not fans of escort missions, our heroes successfully pulled it off in time to travel... to the Triassic!

*The size of this graphic novel's dinosaurs are exaggerated, and do not really represent the true sizes of the creatures. Hey, it makes for a more visually exciting story!

CHAPTER 1
TRIASSIC TRANSPORT

AREN'T WE BACK TO THE FUTURE YET?!

OH, NO! HE'S LOST IT! AGAIN!

WE'RE NEVER GOING HOME...! GOODBYE, MOM AND DAD! GOOD--

FHOOSH!

SHUFF

I BUILT THIS, OUT OF SCRAP!

I CALL IT "DIVVY"! IT'S DESIGNED SO THAT EVEN CHILDREN CAN DRIVE IT!

Amazing!

Whoa!

Ha!

BEEP

AND LOOK! ALL SORTS OF ACTUAL DINOSAURS ARE RUNNING AROUND! LOOK, THERE'S ONE NOW!

NOPE! STILL NOTHING!

KRK

WHY DON'T YOU LET ME--

I'LL DO IT...

OUT OF MY WAY...!

WHOA, WHOA! EASY THERE!

MACHINE SPIRITS...

HEAR MY PLEA...

VROOM

YES!

Hee!

VROOM

YAHAHA

YO! SOMEONE PUT ON "BORN TO BE WILD"!

EMILY, STOP IT! YOU'RE SCARING ME!

HERE THEY GO AGAIN!

@#%*!

THIS IS GOING TO BE A RUNNING THEME, ISN'T IT?

VROOM

OH, HEY, WE'RE NOT DEAD, AND THEY'RE NOT DEAD. HOW ABOUT THAT? HA! HA!

LOOK WHAT YOU'VE DONE, EMILY! IF I HADN'T TAKEN THE WHEEL, WE'D HAVE RUN THEM OVER!

LIKE YOU'RE A BETTER DRIVER!

HOW WAS I SUPPOSED TO DRIVE WITH YOU BUGGING ME?!

HEH! SOME "DRIVER" YOU ARE!

Meh!

Come on, you two...

Argh...

During the Triassic, the only land on Earth was the supercontinent "Pangaea," which was located at the equator and connected the North and South Pole. A narrow sea separated what would be today's North American and European continents, and the Tethys Ocean submerged much of the European continent. Through the Mid-Triassic period, the shape of the modern world gradually became more evident, hinting of the split of the Pangaean supercontinent.

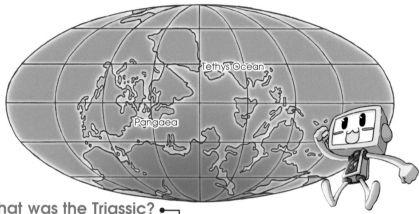

What was the Triassic?

The Triassic was the seventh period in the Earth's geological time scale, and the first of the Mesozoic era. This era began approximately 250 million years ago and ended around 203 million years ago. Additionally, this era was marked by two mass extinctions which occurred just before the Permian-Triassic extinction event and right after the Late Triassic extinction event. There was also a great change in the environment due to the super continent slowly separating. The vast global Panthalassic Ocean surrounded the supercontinent of Pangaea, and was thought to be larger than all oceans of today combined.

I SHALL CALL IT-- **THE TRIASSIC!**

Origin of the name "Triassic"

In 1834 the German geologist Friedrich August Von Alberti named the period after the three geological layers present in sedimentary deposits throughout northern Europe.

Was the environment of Pangaea suitable for plants?

Only the coastal areas; due to its huge expanse of land, winds from the sea were unable to carry moisture deeper into the interior. As a result, the center of Pangaea was largely desert, and compared to other geological eras, the climate was much warmer and drier. As continents combined, what were once originally coastal areas became land, stranding many marine creatures. While Pangaea's general environment worsened over time, however, stronger creatures prevailed, eventually evolving to fill the niches extinct species had left behind, populating the Triassic with new life forms.

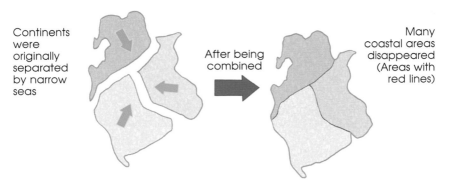

Continents were originally separated by narrow seas

After being combined

Many coastal areas disappeared (Areas with red lines)

What plants existed in the Triassic?

Most of the plants in the previous era went extinct in the Triassic; it was a time when evergreen plants thrived. In areas close to the sea and with ample amounts of rain, one would have discovered large quantities of ferns which gave way in the late Triassic to cycads, conifers, and ginkgoaceae. Furthermore, flowering plants (angiosperms) began to appear during this period.

What could be found in the Triassic sea?

During the Triassic, the first modern corals appeared, forming small reefs. Prehistoric marine creatures were eventually replaced by the Actinopterygii, early sharks, and rays. As for marine reptiles, the ichthyosaurs of the Triassic had adapted to underwater life, capable of surviving in the sea for long periods of time.

The Triassic occurred between two mass extinctions; was it a hard place to live?

Though many species died off in the Late Permian mass extinction, stronger species prevailed. Indeed, by sheer virtue of survival, these species were now able to withstand more demanding environments, becoming the early ancestors of modern life. As for the Late Triassic mass extinction, though many species died out, this also left the Earth bare enough to accommodate dinosaurs.

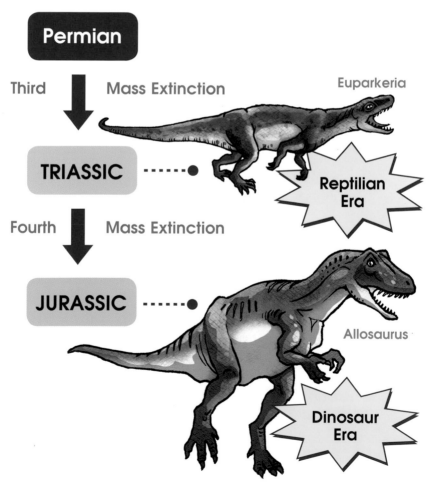

Permian

Third   Mass Extinction   Euparkeria

TRIASSIC ......●   Reptilian Era

Fourth   Mass Extinction

JURASSIC ......●   Allosaurus

Dinosaur Era

Did the terrifying Dimetrodon survive the Triassic?

Unfortunately not. Most of the land vertebrates of the Permian, including the Dimetrodon, disappeared after the Permian-Triassic extinction event. Nevertheless, the Triassic remained an era of reptiles, with many signs of their existence. Not only did early crocodiles and tortoises begin evolving, but pterosaurs and other dinosaur species as well.

Did the dinosaurs appear in the Triassic?

Yes, the dinosaurs finally emerged in the Triassic Era. The climate and environment, however, were quite singular, not enough to drive dinosaurs into different routes of evolution. Hence, there were only few dinosaur species during this era and their sizes were not comparable to those that emerged later. Truly gigantic dinosaurs and a wide variety of species only appeared in the late Triassic.

Similar dinosaurs of the Triassic

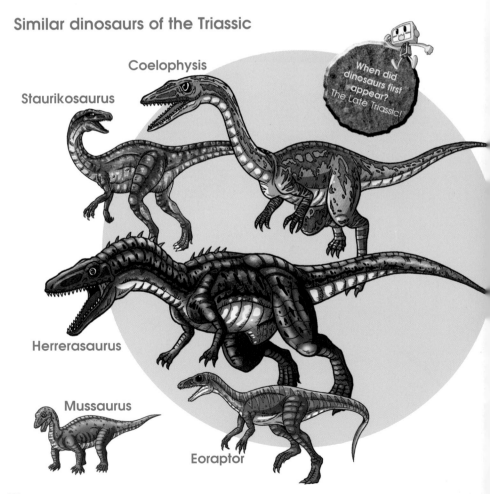

Coelophysis

Staurikosaurus

When did dinosaurs first appear? The Late Triassic!

Herrerasaurus

Mussaurus

Eoraptor

CHAPTER 2
ROCK OF AGES

EMILY, WAIT! YOU CAN'T WANDER OFF ALONE! NOT HERE!

FORGET HER, *STONE!* WE'VE GOT WORK TO DO! SHE'LL BE ALRIGHT.

I MEAN, IT'S NOT LIKE SHE'S THREE YEARS OLD... SHE'LL FIND HER WAY BACK!

Whoa!

RAIN, EITHER YOU'RE HEARTLESS AND DON'T CARE WHAT HAPPENS, OR YOU'RE BRAINLESS AND HAVE NO IDEA OF THE DANGER! EITHER WAY, I DON'T LIKE IT.

H-HEY, STONE? RELAX, BIG GUY!

DO YOU REALIZE THE KIND OF DANGER EMILY MIGHT BE WALKING INTO, THANKS TO YOU?! YOU BETTER APOLOGIZE TO HER NOW!

Y-YOU'RE WRONG! IT'S ALL EMILY'S FAULT! WHY DO I HAVE TO--

FINE. HAVE IT YOUR WAY.

IF YOU'LL EXCUSE ME, I HAVE A FRIEND TO BRING BACK.

AND I'M TAKING LIL S WITH ME!

LIL S?! YOU'RE GOING WITH HIM?! TRAITOR!

WHATEVER, RAIN!

DOESN'T CHANGE THE FACT THAT YOU LEFT EMILY TO FACE THE TRIASSIC ALONE! I'M VERY DISAPPOINTED IN YOU! I'M GOING TO HELP STONE FIND HER!

Nngh...!

FINE, HAVE IT YOUR WAY! I DON'T CARE WHAT HAPPENS TO YOU GUYS! IT DOESN'T BOTHER ME, NOT ONE BIT! I HOPE YOU HAVE FUN OUT THERE, HAH!

THAT'S WEIRD! ISN'T THIS THE PART WHERE THEY COME RUNNING AFTER ME?

Eh?

NYERK!

SNAP

So cute!

AWW, YOU LOOK SO CUTE, EVEN WHEN YOU'RE TRYING TO BITE ME!

PASH

NOW WE HAVE TWO OF YOU...

OH, THERE ARE FOUR...

TEN...

NOT CUTE! NOT CUTE AT--AAAIIEE!

SSHHAK

Don't worry, Emily! Help is here!

OH, IT'S JUST YOU...

?!

CHOMP

Phew!

LOOKS LIKE IT SAVED US!

NRK?

What?!

No way!

GUESS YOU SPOKE TOO SOON!

KREAAAAH!

FWOOSH

WAK

EMILY, TAKE LIL S AND RUN! HE'LL LEAD YOU BACK!

WHAT ABOUT YOU?!

I'LL BE FINE! JUST RUN!

They're gaining on us!

EEEP!

HOLD ON!

FWOOOSH

KREEEAH!

Thrinaxodon possessed attributes of both mammals and reptiles. It had incisors, canines, and molars with a jutting snout and a body that could have possibly been covered with fur. Its chest and lower back were divided by a diaphragm to help its breathing. Based on all these characteristics, it has been suggested that Thrinaxodon was closely related to early mammal ancestors.

Scientific name: Thrinaxodon
Length: 12 to 20 inches
Diet: Small animals
Habitat: Shallow burrows
Discovered: South Africa, South Pole
Era: Early Triassic

Scientific name: Massetognathus
Length: 20 feet
Diet: Plants
Habitat: Unknown
Discovered: America
Era: Middle Triassic

Massetognathus was a long-snouted creature that belonged to the clade Cynodontia. Apart from incisors and canine teeth, it also had blunt molars, suitable for grinding food. Its clawed feet were similar to those of a dog, and its overall appearance was mammal-like.

TAKING IN THE TRIASSIC
Eozostrodon

Eozostrodon was one of the earliest known mammals; despite the fact that it laid eggs, females still used milk glands to feed their young— a major mammal trait. It was thought to have had fur on its body as well. Its teeth were typically mammalian, heavy, and sharpened. Today, paleontologists opine that its large eyes indicated that it could have been a nocturnal.

Scientific name: Eozostrodon
Length: 3 inches
Diet: Insects and other small animals
Habitat: Forests
Discovered: West Europe, South Africa
Era: Late Triassic to Early Jurassic

TAKING IN THE TRIASSIC
Placerias

Placerias was one of the last existing dicynodonts during the Late Triassic. Its most notable features were its beak-like mouth and the protruding tusks which helped in chewing tough vegetation. Its tusks could also be used for digging, allowing it to reach the water-filled roots of ferns.

Scientific name: Placerias
Length: 10 feet
Diet: Vegetation
Habitat: In the wild
Discovered: America
Era: Late Triassic

Lystrosaurus were one of the very few species that survived the mass extinction during the Late Permian. They spread all over the world in the early Triassic, and some scientists estimate that there might have been a billion of them in existence. Due to their vast numbers, they were often used as important evidence to support the theory of continental drift.

Scientific name: Lystrosaurus
Length: 3 feet
Diet: Vegetation
Habitat: Close to water plants
Discovered: South Pole, South Africa, India, China, and Russia
Era: Late Permian to Early Triassic

Longisquama was a controversial prehistoric animal; its single fossilized skeleton (itself incomplete) shows five improperly preserved appendages protruding from its back. This caused much debate among paleontologists, some competing theories include suggestions that the appendages were scales, feathers and even ludicrously, fern leaves which somehow got mixed in with the rest of the fossil. If they really were feathers, Longisquama could be the key to discovering when dinosaurs evolved into birds. Unfortunately, until an intact fossil can be found, the answer remains undetermined.

Scientific name: Longisquama
Length: 6 inches
Diet: Unknown
Habitat: Unknown
Discovered: Central Asia
Era: Middle to Late Triassic

TAKING IN THE TRIASSIC
Hypsognathus

Scientific name: Hypsognathus
Length: 12 inches
Diet: Vegetation
Habitat: Unknown
Discovered: America
Era: Late Triassic

The lizardlike Hypsognathus was not closely related to its latter day counterpart. It had a low, short body with a relatively short tail. A notable feature was the frill of spikes on either side of its head, which was thought to be used as a defense to ward off predators.

TAKING IN THE TRIASSIC
Mastodonsaurus

Scientific name: Mastodonsaurus
Length: 7 feet
Diet: Vegetation
Habitat: Unknown
Discovered: America
Era: Middle Triassic

Mastodonsaurus (its name meant "breast tooth lizard"), had a long powerful head with short, stout limbs, but its most interesting characteristic were the two triangular tusks which slotted through the openings on its palate and projected through the top of its snout when its jaws were closed.

TAKING IN THE TRIASSIC
Aeger

Aeger had 10 legs, long antennae, and a tail. Physically, it bore close resemblance to modern prawns.

Scientific name: Aeger
Length: 5 inches
Diet: Unknown
Habitat: Unknown
Discovered: Around the world
Era: Triassic to Jurassic

GOING FASTER!

SEAN, THINK OF SOMETHING! QUICK!

COME ON, MANUAL! DON'T LET ME DOWN!

THERE HAS TO BE SOMETHING!

FLIP

WHAM

FORGET THE MANUAL! WE NEED TO TRY SOMETHING NOW!

BEEP

RAIN, WHAT DID YOU PRESS?! LET ME HANDLE THIS!

BEEP

Oh, my...

THIS IS BETTER THAN ANY CHEAPO MASSAGE CHAIR!

You're the best!

Good job, Prof!

BUT THIS IS NOT THE TIME! I'M GONNA TRY MORE BUTTONS!

WHAT? FORGET IT! KEEP YOUR PAWS OFF THO--

WE'VE GOT TO FIND A WAY TO SHAKE HIM OFF!

WUMP

UW AAH!

It's here!

SKIISH

SKIISH

SKIISH

SKREET

FLOP

Aha!

FZZZAP

We made it...!

OI! WHAT'S THE BIG IDEA?!

SORRY! IT CAUSES A SHOCK APPARENTLY!

AH, AT LEAST WE'RE SAFE NOW! THAT WAS TOO CLOSE!

RAIN...

IT JUST HIT ME... WE HAVE DIVVY THE "SUPERCAR" AND YET WE BARELY ESCAPED WITH OUR LIVES...

CAN YOU IMAGINE WHAT COULD HAPPEN TO STONE AND EMILY?

Huh?

AND THIS IS ALL YOUR FAULT! THEY'RE OUT THERE BECAUSE OF YOU!

MOVE OVER! WE MUST FIND THEM!

Gah!

?!

SEAN, IS THAT YOUR GIRLY SHOE?

NO! I HAVEN'T STEPPED OUT OF THIS CAR, YOU MORON! IT'S OBVIOUSLY EM--

...Emily?!

N-NAH, YOU'RE OVERTHINKING IT! IT'S PROBABLY THE DINOSAUR'S! THEY'RE SMART, THEY CAN MAKE IT THEMSELVES!

HOW SMART DO YOU THINK A DINOSAUR CAN GET? AND WHY, PRAY TELL, WOULD THEY NEED SHOES?!

UH, MAYBE AN ALIEN MADE THEM... OR SOMETHING...

I HAVE TO SAVE RAIN!

OH, FOR-- START UP ALREADY!

Hurry!

RAIN, BEHIND YOU! RUN!

The superorder Dinosauria (basically, a general term for all dinosaurs) was divided into the two suborders; Saurischians (lizard-hipped) and Ornithischians (bird-hipped). The differences between the two groups were the bone structures of their pelvises.

Saurischia

Viewing it from the side, the Saurischians's pelvis structure had a three-pronged shape, with the pubic bone extending forward underneath the ilium while the ischium pointed backwards. This structure is similar to that of reptiles!

SAURISCHIA

Prosauropods

Prosauropods such as Plateosaurus were a group of small to mid-sized dinosaurs that lived during the Late Triassic. They had sturdy bodies and could walk on two legs (bipedal).
Era: Late Triassic.
Completely extinct by
the Early Jurassic.

Plateosaurus

Sauropodomorphs

Sauropodomorphs evolved from the Prosauropods and most of them were large herbivores. Their common characteristics included their small heads, long necks and tails and spatula-like teeth.
Era: Jurassic to Cretaceous

Diplodocus

Theropods

Theropods were not only the earliest, but also the most successfully evolved dinosaurs. They were bipedal with long sharp claws, and sharp jagged teeth with serrated edges.
Era: Late Triassic to Cretaceous

Tyrannosaurus
rex

Ornithischia

For the Ornithischians, their ilium was greatly expanded with their pubis jutting forward. Looking at it from the side, their bones seemed to extend in four directions. These bones can be divided into the front and back halves of the ilium; one part of the pubic bone was connected to the ischium while the back and other parts of the pubic bone provided support.

Ornithopods

Ornithopod fossils comprise the vast majority of fossils discovered. They were all herbivores, with some being bipedal and others quadruped.
Era: Late Triassic to Cretaceous

Iguanodon

Stegosauria

Stegosaurs were herbivores which first appeared during the Jurassic, lasting until the early Cretaceous. They walked on all fours with a series of straight plates and spines on their humped backs, and also had a pair of spikes near the end of their tails.
Period: Jurassic to Early Cretaceous

Stegosaurus

Ankylosaurus

Ankylosaurs were dinosaurs with short, sturdy bodies covered in heavy plate armor. They had four short limbs, with their hind limbs longer than their front limbs, causing them to move slowly.
Era: Cretaceous

Hylaeosaurus

Ceratopsia

Ceratopsids were dinosaurs exclusive to the Cretaceous Era. The back of their skull flared out rearwards, extending the parietal and squamosal bones of the skull roof to form a neck frill which was triangular-shaped.
Era: Cretaceous

Triceratops

Pachycephalosauria

The most notable pachycephalosaur features were their thick dome-shaped skulls and closed temporal holes. Their pubic bones were crowded out by their ischiums, forming their acetabulums.
Era: Cretaceous

Pachycephalo-saurus

ORNITHISCHIA

Lagosuchus

Lagosuchus was similar in size to modern day rabbits, but its body was much lighter. It had long hind limbs with calves longer than its thighs and splayed feet for support. This granted it the speed needed to capture its prey. Paleontologists believed that Logosuchus could possibly be among the dinosaur's earliest ancestors.

Scientific name: Lagosuchus
Length: 12 inches
Diet: Other animals
Habitat: Forests
Discovered: South Africa
Era: Mid-Triassic

Euparkeria

Scientific name: Euparkeria
Length: 2 feet
Diet: Other animals
Habitat: Forests
Discovered: South Africa
Era: Early Triassic

Even though Euparkeria was closely related to the early dinosaurs, it was categorized as an archosauriform. Its front and hind limbs were huge, and its tail comprised more than half its entire length. This caused some paleontologists to suggest it relied on its hind limbs to speed up, and straightened its tail to balance its body. Euparkeria usually travelled on all fours, but is still currently regarded as one of the forefathers of bipedal reptiles.

Mussaurus

Mussaurus was recognized as one of the earliest dinosaurs and its fossil remains were also some of the smallest; all fossils discovered so far have measured between 8 to 15 inches. As such, they are suspected to be the remains of newly birthed hatchlings. Some paleontologists estimate that the Mussaurus could have reached a length of up to 10 feet.

Scientific name: Mussaurus
Length: 8 to 15 inches (currently known)
Diet: Herbivore
Habitat: Unknown
Discovered: Argentina
Era: Late Triassic

Lufengosaurus

Lufengosaurus was one of the first complete dinosaur fossils to be discovered in China. It was a mid-sized prosauropod dinosaur that measured around 7 feet upright—about the size of modern–day horses. It had a small head and forelimbs that were half the length of its hind limbs indicating it could have been primarily bipedal.

Scientific name: Lufengosaurus
Length: 20 feet
Diet: Herbivore
Habitat: Forest
Discovered: China
Era: Late Triassic to Early Jurassic

Wait! Maybe—

LIL S! DO YOU COPY?!

I FORGOT HE COULD COMMUNICATE WITH LIL S VIA HIS BADGE! BUT...

IT'S ALL MY FAULT! I SENT EMILY AND STONE TO THEIR DEATHS!

NO REPLY! THIS ISN'T WORKING EITHER!

Urgh...

QUIT MOPING, RAIN! YOU WANT TO MAKE THINGS BETTER, THEN HELP OUT INSTEAD!

AND THAT SHOE PROVES NOTHING!

HAVE FAITH! AS LONG AS THERE ISN'T A BODY, THERE'S HOPE THEY'RE ALIVE!

TOOLS, TOOLS, TOOLS...

RAIN, SNAP OUT OF IT! I NEED A HAND!

HEY, DID YOU HEAR ME? RAIN!

RUSTLE

HEY, SAY SOMETHING!

HUH? WHAT'S THIS?

THESE ARE TOO SMALL!

THERE'S NOTHING USEFUL HERE!

GRR

What the-- ?!

HUH?

SEAN! NO!

FZZAP

FZZAP

...

ANYWAY, THE THING IS...

I THINK EMILY AND STONE ARE STILL ALIVE!

WHAT?! HAVE YOU FORGOTTEN THE PAST FEW MIN--?!

NO, REALLY! SEE?

THAT HAS TO BE THEM! THEY'RE STILL ALIVE!

IT'S A SMOKE SIGNAL! THEY'RE PROBABLY USING IT TO SIGNAL FOR HELP! C'MON!

Smoke signal?

VROOM

TAKING IN THE TRIASSIC

Eoraptor

Eoraptor lunensis, which means "dawn plunderer from the Valley of the Moon," earned its fanciful name as a result of where its first fossil was discovered, in north-western Argentina. It was one of the earliest carnivorous dinosaurs, and its discovery changed views on when dinosaurs first appeared. It was not exceptionally large, but had strong hind limbs which helped it chase prey while its forelimbs had sharp claws which would have been powerful enough to capture and overpower creatures of similiar size.

The Eoraptor had jagged sharp teeth on both sides of its inner jaw, a predatory attribute. On the other hand, it also possessed leaf-shaped teeth—implying a herbivorous capacity, leading to its classification as an omnivore.

Scientific name: Eoraptor
Length: 3 feet
Diet: Other animals
(Some theories suggest it was an omnivore)
Habitat: Forests
Discovered: Argentina
Era: Mid Triassic

Which was the first dinosaur?

The answer will continue to change as new species are discovered. In the mid-20th century, it was generally believed that Coelophysis was the earliest dinosaur, but this theory was debunked after the discovery of the Herrerasaurus when a complete fossil was excavated in the late 90s. In 1993, the Eoraptor was unearthed, and the current theory is that both Herrerasaurus and Eoraptor were the earliest dinosaurs.

Coelophysis

Coelophysis was one of the earliest known dinosaurs; its name means "hollow form," referring to its hollow bones, similiar to a bird's, making it incredibly light, capable of easily outrunning heavier prey and its predators. It had similar attributes to smaller animals, and relied on its powerful hind limbs to sprint. When running, it tucked in its fore limbs to its chest and raised its tail to maintain its balance.

Which was the first real dinosaur? It's a tie: The Herrerasaurus and Eoraptor.

Scientific name: Coelophysis
Length: 10 feet
Diet: Other animals
Habitat: Desert plain
Discovered: America and South Africa
Era: Late Triassic

COELOPHYSIS BONE STRUCTURE

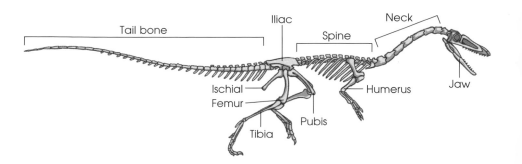

Tail bone — Iliac — Spine — Neck — Ischial — Femur — Pubis — Tibia — Humerus — Jaw

CHAPTER 5
TO THE RESCUE

I REMEMBER THIS BAG. STONE WAS CARRYING IT WHEN HE LEFT THE CAR...

WHERE DID THEY GO?

I THINK THEY MIGHT BE NEARBY...

YES, I'M CERTAIN THEY'RE ALIVE. JUST LOOK AT THOSE FOOTPRINTS!

BACK TO THE CAR! IF WE TRACK THEIR FOOTPRINTS, WE'LL COME ACROSS THEM SOON ENOUGH!

STONE, EMILY, HANG IN THERE! WE'RE COMING FOR YOU!

YEAH, THEY CAN'T BE FAR!

WE SHOULD HEAD TOWARDS THE SMOKE SIGNAL...

What?

SMOKE SIGNAL? LOOKS LIKE NORMAL SMOKE TO ME...

WHAT DO YOU MEAN? IT MIGHT BE THE THING THAT SAVES YOUR LIFE IN A TIME OF NEED!

HUH?

DID YOU KNOW THAT ONE OF THE BEST DAYTIME EMERGENCY SIGNALS IS THICK SMOKE?!

First, build a fire. Then, place some dry leaves and branches on top of it to produce white smoke.

Next, wet your jacket, shirt, or towel if possible. If you can't find water, ignore this step. Place the garment above the fire, pause for a while and remove it, then repeat.

HERE WE GO AGAIN...

Repeat the action three times, quickly...

The rising smoke will be separated into three "puffs." This is the standard code for emergencies. Repeat this until help arrives.

HUH? THE SMOKE IS DIFFERENT FROM BEFORE...

What?

THEY MIGHT BE IN DANGER! WE'VE GOT TO REACH THEM FAST!

VROOM

Urgh...

GRR!

CRACK

CRACK

STONE! IT'S ALL YOUR FAULT! FRYING THE FISH ATTRACTED THEM!

THE FIRE WAS TO SIGNAL OUR LOCATION, NOT FOR A PICNIC!

I WAS HUNGRY... AND IT WAS ONLY A LITTLE!

WHAT DO WE DO NOW?!

IF RAIN WERE HERE, HE WOULD PROBABLY COME UP WITH SOMETHING!

IF YOU MENTION THAT HEARTLESS JERK ONE MORE TIME, YOU'RE ON YOUR OWN!

BZZT

LUCKILY, THE PROFESSOR INVENTED THIS SHIELD THAT COULD WITHSTAND DINOSAUR ATTACKS!

BZZZT

CRACK

OH, NO!

STONE, WE'VE GOT TO THINK OF SOMETHING! THE SHIELD IS FAILING!

I'M NOT THE "GO TO" GUY, I'M THE "FIX IT" GUY!

WAIT! AS SOON AS THE SHIELD FALLS, JUST RUN! DON'T LOOK BACK, JUST RUN AS FAST YOU CAN!

STONE... DO YOU...

What?!

DO YOU HONESTLY THINK I WOULD AGREE TO THIS STUPID "PLAN" OF YOURS?! I WILL NEVER LEAVE A FRIEND BEHIND TO SAVE MY OWN SKIN!

IF WE'RE GOING TO RUN, WE'RE DOING IT TOGETHER!

UH, RIGHT!

GET READY GUYS!

KRASH

MOVE IT!

GRAAAH!

102

RAIN, WHAT ARE YOU DOING? WHY ARE YOU TURNING BACK?!

SKREECH

BEFORE WE LEAVE, THERE'S ONE MORE THING THAT NEEDS TO BE DONE-- NO, TWO.

FIRST IS, WELL, ...

I'M SORRY, EMILY! I WAS STUPID AND ANGRY AND I RAN MY MOUTH OFF AND I'M SORRY!

HMPH!

I SWEAR I'LL NEVER DO THAT TO YOU AGAIN!

Geez, I...

HELLO?! BIG NASTY THAT THINKS WE'RE REAL TASTY APPROACHING REAL HASTY!

VRRRM

RAIN, WHAT THE HECK ARE YOU DOING?!

105

THE PRESTOSUCHUS MEASURED SIXTEEN FEET, AND WAS MOSTLY AN AMBUSH PREDATOR. ITS STRONG, STURDY LEGS ALLOWED IT TO MOVE QUICKLY.

WE... WE ACTUALLY BEAT IT!

Rocky, eat your heart out!!

No way!

HRM!

Proterosuchus

Proterosuchus was one of the largest predatory land reptiles of the Triassic. Its body was massive and heavy and even though it shared similiar characteristics and lifestyle with modern crocodiles, paleontologists do not believe both species are directly related and that it was a coincidence they shared similiar lifestyles. If anything, it only proved that Proterosuchus was a primitive species with a splayed four-legged movement pattern.

Scientific name: Proterosuchus
Length: 10 feet
Diet: Other animals
Habitat: Coast, swamp
Discovered: China and South Africa
Era: Early Triassic

Desmatosuchus

Scientific name: Desmatosuchus
Length: 16 feet
Diet: Herbivore
Habitat: Forest
Discovered: North America
Era: Mid to Late Triassic

Desmatosuchus had short limbs, but a long tail and body covered in bony plate armor. It had a pair of 1 foot horns on the back of its shoulders along with two rows of spikes. The Desmatosuchus might have looked fierce and dangerous, but its formidable armor was purely defensive.

Parasuchus

Parasuchus was an amphibious predator that belonged to the order Phytosauria. It was closely related to crocodiles, its whole body was covered with thick scales with an underside supported by strong ribs. Furthermore, with nostrils situated on the top of its snout like modern crocodiles, it could submerge while keeping its nose above the surface to breathe—as modern crocodiles do.

Scientific name: Parasuchus
Length: 8 feet
Diet: Fish
Habitat: Coast, swamp
Discovered: India
Era: Mid to Late Triassic

What were the Archosauria?
The Archosauria, the archosaur clade, is a group of diapsid amniotes whose living representatives include birds and crocodilians.

Prestosuchus

Even though its body shape and upright posture resembled that of dinosaurs', it actually belonged to the order Archosauria. With strong limbs, it could sprint at high speed, making Prestosuchus one of the most fearsome predators during the Triassic.

Scientific name: Prestosuchus
Length: 17 to 23 feet
Diet: Other animals
Habitat: Coast
Discovered: Brazil
Era: Late Triassic

Prestosuchus skull

The Prestosaurus had a long pair of jaws with jagged teeth.

CHAPTER 6
OCEAN OVERLOAD

SPLOOSH

GAH!

BEEP

FWOOP

SHTINK

SHONISAURUS SWAM IN THE LATE TRIASSIC SEA AND IS ONE OF THE LARGEST ICHTHYOSAURUS TO BE DISCOVERED SO FAR.

ITS WHALE-LIKE BODY TAPERED INTO A LONG, THIN TOOTH-LINED SNOUT AND POWERFUL FINS.

PALEONTOLOGISTS ONCE DISCOVERED A 75 FEET LONG FOSSIL OF AN ICHTHYOSAUR IN COLOMBIA!

LET'S GET OUT OF HERE, RAIN! THIS IS MUCH TOO CLOSE!

WAK

VRRRRM

WAIT! THAT CANYON-- WE MIGHT BE ABLE TO SQUEEZE THROUGH!

ONE THING'S FOR SURE, THAT BIG BULLY WON'T!

HAH! NOW WE'RE SAFE!

ATTENTION! WATER PRESSURE SYSTEMS HAVE BEEN ACTIVATED!

WATER PRESSURE SYSTEM... ON

WATER PRESSURE? IS THAT LIKE BLOOD PRESSURE?

Gwah...

Water pressure refers to the pressure in water. To illustrate this, we can conduct an experiment to see water pressure in action. First, fill a barrel with water and then poke three holes at a height of 1 inch, 1.5 inches, and 2 inches above the ground.

Results?:
The water from the 1 inch hole will expel water the farthest, followed by the 1.5 inches hole, with the water spurting from the 2 inches hole closest to the barrel.

Basically, the deeper the water, the higher the pressure, due to all the water above it.

2-inches

1.5-inches

1-inch

KRAK

WHAT?

CREEEAK

PLIP

HEY, GUYS! WE CAN'T GO ANY DEEPER! THE CAR CAN'T TAKE MUCH MORE!

IF WE CONTINUE DOWNWARDS, WE'LL BE CRUSHED! HURRY, HEAD BACK UP!

RAIN, LIGHTS OFF! YOU'LL ATTRACT SOMETHING NASTY!

SORRY! WRONG BUTTON!

Huh? That's--

LET'S JUST OBSERVE THE SITUATION AT THIS DEPTH AND SEE HOW IT GOES!

WARNING! NOTHOSAURUS APPROACHING!

NOTHO-- WHAT NOW?!

NOTHOSAURUS WAS A SEMI-OCEANIC CREATURE WITH SHARP NEEDLE TEETH.

MEASURING ABOUT 13 FEET, IT IS ONE OF THE EARLIEST KNOWN PLESIOSAURIUS. IT USED ITS FOUR LONG LEGS, WEBBED FEET AND MIGHTY TAIL TO PROPEL ITSELF FORWARD UNDERWATER.

SHRAAAH!

SNAP

SNAP

OH, GREAT, LOOK WHO SHOWED UP!

WHOA! THEY'RE ATTACKING EACH OTHER!

HUH-- THE NOTHOSAURUS MIGHT BE SMALLER, BUT IT'S FASTER TOO!

MAYBE IT'S TRYING TO TIRE ITS OPPONENT OUT, THEN GO FOR THE KILL!

RRRIP

LOOK, THE SHONISAURUS IS TRYING TO ESCAPE!

CHOMP

SHRRRP

LOOKS LIKE THE LITTLE GUY WON THIS ONE! I DIDN'T SEE THAT COMING!

Nothosaurus

Nothosaurus shared similar physical attributes to modern crocodiles, such as long, tapering jaws with intercrossing teeth that allowed it to clamp down on prey. Nothosaurus mostly remained underwater, using its sinuous body and flexible tail to propel it through the water; its four webbed feet were only used to increase speed and maneuvrability when hunting.

Did the Nothosaurus live underwater all their life? Nope! Like turtles and crocodiles, they laid their eggs at the beach.

Scientific name: Nothosaurus
Length: Roughly 20 feet
Diet: Fish and prawns
Habitat: Coast
Discovered: Europe
Era: Triassic

Cymbospondylus

Scientific name: Cymbospondylus
Length: 33 feet
Diet: Other animals
Habitat: Ocean
Discovered: North America, South America, Europe and China
Era: Early to Mid-Triassic

Cymbospondylus's name means "Boat Spine," It resembled modern dolphins, and was a marine creature that lived and reproduced in the sea. The ichthyosaurs of this era did not have fins; instead, they relied on their four limbs and long tail fin to navigate underwater.

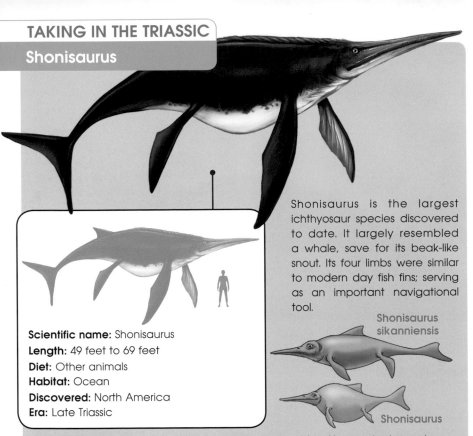

Shonisaurus is the largest ichthyosaur species discovered to date. It largely resembled a whale, save for its beak-like snout. Its four limbs were similar to modern day fish fins; serving as an important navigational tool.

Shonisaurus sikanniensis

Shonisaurus

Scientific name: Shonisaurus
Length: 49 feet to 69 feet
Diet: Other animals
Habitat: Ocean
Discovered: North America
Era: Late Triassic

Most Shonisaurs measured about 49 feet and were considered large animals even by the standards of the Triassic ocean. In recent years, however, a new species, Shonisaurus sikanniensis, was found—it boasted a 69 feet, making it the new overlord of the ocean.

Himalayesaurus

Himalayasaurus was first discovered at the "roof of the world," (the Himalayas). Paleontologists suspect that it might be related to the Shonisaurus. In any case, these fossils prove that the Himalayas were once underwater during the Triassic.

Himalayasaurus, which once dwelled in the Triassic ocean, is now a fossil beneath the Himalayan mountains.

Henodus

Henodus's body was covered by a carapace, much like modern day tortoises. Its back and belly had horn-plated scales which protected it from larger predators. It did not have teeth, but its lower and upper jaws formed hard beaks, which allowed it to pry shellfish off rocks and crush them in its mouth.

Scientific name: Henodus
Length: 3 feet
Diet: Shellfish
Habitat: Coral reefs
Discovered: Europe
Era: Late Triassic

Are the Henodus and Psephoderma early ancestors of the tortoise? Even though they shared similar attributes, these two species are not related to the modern tortoise.

Psephoderma

Scientific name: Psephoderma
Length: 3 feet
Diet: Conches and crustaceans
Habitat: Shallow waters
Discovered: Europe
Era: Late Triassic

Psephoderma had a carapace, but unlike most of its kind, its shell was divided into two parts: one to protect the back and belly, while the other guarded its rear end. Furthermore, its carapace was shaped unevenly with its body being flat and large. It had rounded teeth in its jaw which allowed it to crush shellfish.

Scientific name: Peteinosaurus
Length: 2 feet
Diet: Flying insects
Habitat: Swamps and valleys
Discovered: Europe
Era: Mid to Late Triassic

Peteinosaurus was an early pterosaur. It had a thin membrane that spread across the fourth digit of its wings, and a sturdy but light bone structure. Given its 2 feet wingspan, it took to the skies quite easily relying on the bones in its long tail to maintain balance.

Comparison with other flying animals

Peteinosaurus
Peteinosaurus had a thin membrane that spread across the fourth digit of its wings.

Bat
The thin membrane on its wings is spread between their second and fifth digit.

Bird
Its wings are covered with feathers.

Even though their wings were similar to those of a bat, the bone structures were quite different, and even more so compared to birds.

Scientific name: Eudimorphodon
Length: 2.5 feet
Diet: Fish
Habitat: Coast
Discovered: Italy
Era: Late Triassic

Eudimorphodon had a wing span of 3 feet and a spade-shaped flap at the end of its tail to help navigate, much like a boat rudder. Even though its head was only 2.5 inches in length, it contained 114 teeth!

CHAPTER 7
DALLYING WITH DANGER!

VROOM

RUSTLE

ACCORDING TO THE RADAR, THE LAB'S RIGHT THIS WAY...

IT IS A PLATEOSAURUS, A GIGANTIC DINOSAUR OF THE "PROSAUROPOD" GROUP. ITS PHYSICAL ATTRIBUTES INCLUDE A SMALL HEAD, LONG NECK, BLUNT SERRATED TEETH FOR CRUSHING LEAVES, STRONG LIMBS WITH LARGE TOES, AND SHARP CLAWS.

VROOM

YIKES! HE'S RIGHT BESIDE US! WE'RE GOING TO BE EATEN!

So huge!

HELLO? "BLUNT SERRATED TEETH FOR CRUSHING LEAVES"!

IT'S A HERBIVORE!

139

OH, HEH, SORRY, WASN'T PAYING ATTENTION. HERBIVORES, EH? THEN WE'RE COOL.

HUH? THEY'RE HEADING IN THE SAME DIRECTION AS WE ARE!

COOL! WE GET A WELCOME HOME PARADE!

BETTER STILL, SUCH A LARGE HERD WOULD BE GREAT FOR SCARING OFF PREDATORS!

RIGHT THEN, LET'S GO!

HOLD ON! IS IT SAFE TO FOLLOW THEM? WHAT IF THEY THINK WE'RE ATTACKING THEM?

HEH! NOT TO WORRY! I HAVE A PLAN!

WELL, NICE TO SEE SOMEONE APPRECIATES YOUR CAMO!

STOP EATING, YOU BIG STUPID LIZARD! I DON'T EAT YOUR STUFF, DO I?!

Do you even HAVE stuff?

Aww, so cute!

I THINK HE LIKES US!

RAIN, STOP THE CAR! I WANT A CLOSER LOOK!

Come! Here are some delicious leaves...!

Come... Come now...!

142

NIBBLE

You like it?

STEAL MY THUNDER, EH!

GO AHEAD! I'VE GOT MY RIDE RIGHT HERE!

C'MON, EM! BACK IN THE CAR BEFORE THEY LEAVE US BEHIND!

VROOM

OH, RAIN... WHAT A PAIN...

YOU JUST HAD TO SHOW ME UP HUH?!

CARE FOR A DINO RIDE, SEAN?

Finally, my turn to drive!

Hohohohoho...

NOPE! I'M MUCH MORE AT HOME ON FOUR WHEELS THANKS!

HEY! THEY'RE HEADING FOR THE OPPOSITE RIVER BANK!

144

ALERT STONE AND SEAN! I'LL GET EMILY!

ROGER THAT! YOU BE CAREFUL!

VVOOSH

HI YAH!

COME ON, BOY! GENTLY DOES IT.

GRR!

CRAAH!

NYEK!

OH, MY... PREDATORS... UHM, NO PRESSURE, BUT IF WE COULD CROSS RIGHT NOW THAT WOULD BE REALLY NICE THANKS...

Eek!

WHACK

WHACK

WHACK

?

?

?

NYEEEK

W-ho...?

EMILY!

RAIN!

WHAT WAS THAT?!

SPLASH

EMILY! ARE YOU OKAY? ARE YOU HURT?

RAIN! WHAT?!

IT'S THE PROFESSOR'S LATEST... THE "BASHARANG"!

NO TIME TO CHAT THOUGH, C'MON!

YOU'RE RIGHT; I DON'T WANT TO TAKE ANY CHANCES! WAIT-- WHAT ABOUT YOU?

NEVER MIND ME, GET GOING!

HEY, YOSHI! IF I FIND A SCRATCH ON EMILY, YOU'RE GONNA GET IT!

YOU DON'T HAVE TO WORRY ABOUT ME! I'VE ALREADY ASKED STONE AND SEAN FOR HELP!

STUPID RAIN! WHAT ABOUT YOU?! YOU BETTER COME BACK OR SO HELP ME I'LL...

GOT-CHA!

TAKING IN THE TRIASSIC

Plateosaurus

Plateosaurus is one of the most famous prosauropods known today, and was one of the largest land dinosaurs of the Triassic. It had a long neck, but a very small head. Powerful hind limbs allowed it to stand upright for short periods of time, and coupled with a long neck, it was able to reach leaves on higher branches with relative ease.

How long does it take food to reach the Plateosaurus's stomach? For humans, food travels at 0.8 to 2 inches per second. If we were to use that as a standard rate, it would take Plateosaurus one minute to swallow its food and 4 minutes for it to reach its belly.

Plateosaurus Bone Structure

Skull
Neck
Spine
Humerus
Radial
Phalanx
Ulna
Femur
Tibia
Tail

Scientific name: Plateosaurus
Length: 26 feet
Diet: Herbivore
Habitat: Plain
Discovered: Europe
Era: Late Triassic

Comparison between dinosaur teeth

Plateosaurs had leaf-shaped teeth which allowed them to eat leaves but not chew them. As such, they had to rely on swallowed stones, called gastroliths, in their stomachs to crush food for digestion.

Plateosaurus's phalanx

Their long and sharp fingers were quite a hindrance while walking, but especially useful as a defensive weapon, and also allowed Plateosaurs to hold onto trees while they fed.

Dimetrodon

Plateosaurus

Diplodocus

Brontosaurus

Stegosaurus

Euskelosaurus was one of the largest prosauropods around, and was closely related to Plateosaurus. The shaft of its thigh bone was twisted outwards, and paleontologists suggest that this was necessary to accommodate food that entered its large belly.

Scientific name: Euskelosaurus
Length: 30 feet
Diet: Herbivore
Habitat: Unknown
Discovered: South Africa
Era: Late Triassic

Jingshanosaurus was one of the last prosauropods to emerge before they were replaced by sauropods. It had an exceptionally long neck which was one-third of its actual height.

Unaysaurus was closely related to Plateosaurus, just much smaller. As they were also discovered in different continents, however, paleontologists believe that plateosaurs migrated across the Pangaean supercontinent from South America to Europe.

Scientific name: Jingshanosaurus
Length: 25 feet
Diet: Herbivore
Habitat: Unknown
Discovered: China
Era: Early Jurassic

Scientific name: Unaysaurus
Length: 8 feet
Diet: Herbivore
Habitat: Unknown
Discovered: Brazil
Era: Late Triassic

CHAPTER 8
'TIL WE MEET AGAIN, TRIASSIC

VVOOSH

FWIP

Yowza!

SNAP

FWOOSH

Gross!

SMOOCH

I KNEW YOU WOULD COME FOR ME!

SKREECH

VRRRM

WE'VE GOT TO GET TO EMILY!

YARK!

GRAAAH!

HYARK!

SHRAAAH!

KREEEAH!

KHA--

CHOMP

SKRCH!

SKRCH!

STONE! WHAT ARE YOU WAITING FOR?

WHAM

LET'S GET OUT OF HERE WHILE THEY'RE KILLING EACH OTHER!

THE HERRERASAURUS WAS A LIGHTLY BUILT HUNTER WITH A LONG TAIL AND RELATIVELY SMALL HEAD.

IT WAS ESTIMATED TO BE AROUND 10 TO 16 FEET WITH A LONG AND NARROW SKULL. IT HAD A FLEXIBLE LOWER JAW WHICH MOVED BACK AND FORTH FOR EASIER BITING.

EMILY! YOSHI AND YOU NEED TO GET OUT OF HERE!

GRRH!

NYAAAARK!

THAT SOUND WAS...

QUICK, CHECK AND SEE IF THERE ARE ANY PLATEOSAURS AROUND!

THERE'S A HERD 66 FEET TO THE WEST!

EMILY, TAKE HIM AND HEAD WEST! THE REST OF THE HERD ARE GATHERED THERE!

GO NOW! ONCE WE'RE DONE, WE'LL CATCH UP WITH YOU!

Guys...

GREAT! HE'S FINALLY BACK WITH HIS FAMILY!

I JUST HOPE STONE... SEAN... RAIN...

EEK?!

VROOOM

SORRY ABOUT THAT! GET IN, WE'RE HEADING HOME!

BOYS!

SEE YOU IN DINOSAUR EXPLORERS #5!

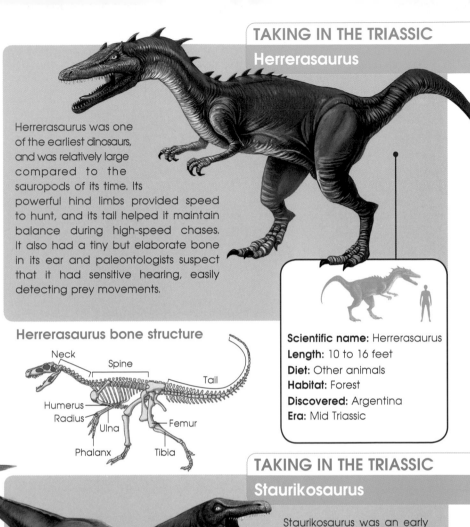

Herrerasaurus was one of the earliest dinosaurs, and was relatively large compared to the sauropods of its time. Its powerful hind limbs provided speed to hunt, and its tail helped it maintain balance during high-speed chases. It also had a tiny but elaborate bone in its ear and paleontologists suspect that it had sensitive hearing, easily detecting prey movements.

Herrerasaurus bone structure

Neck
Spine
Tail
Humerus
Radius
Ulna
Femur
Phalanx
Tibia

Scientific name: Herrerasaurus
Length: 10 to 16 feet
Diet: Other animals
Habitat: Forest
Discovered: Argentina
Era: Mid Triassic

TAKING IN THE TRIASSIC
Staurikosaurus

Staurikosaurus was an early therapod. It had a small but light body with long powerful hind limbs which effectively made it a speedy hunter.

Scientific name: Staurikosaurus
Length: 7 feet
Diet: Other animals
Habitat: Forest and bushes
Discovered: South America
Era: Late Triassic

Gojirasaurus

Named after Godzilla, Gojirasaurus was one of the largest predatory dinosaurs of the Triassic, closely resembling Coelophysis. Some paleontologists, however, doubt its existence as a credible species, and no complete fossil, set has yet been found.

Scientific name: Gojirasaurus
Length: 18 feet
Diet: Other animals
Habitat: Unknown
Discovered: America
Era: Late Triassic

Eocursor

The "dawn runner" was one of the very few bipedal herbivores of the Triassic Era. Its tibia was longer than its femur, and coupled with a naturally light body, it could easily outrun predators. Whether it was its physical form or bone structure, it shared many qualities with the Jurassic Ornithischia, which led paleontologists to believe that the Eocursor could possibly be a precursor of Ornithischia.

Scientific name: Eocursor
Length: 3 feet
Diet: Herbivore
Habitat: Unknown
Discovered: South Africa
                   and America
Era: Late Triassic

Scientific name: Thecodontosaurus
Length: 7 feet
Diet: Herbivore (Some omnivore)
Habitat: Dry highlands or desert plains
Discovered: America
Era: Late Triassic

Thecodontosaurus was one of the earliest discovered prosauropods. Its name means "socket-tooth" lizard, as its teeth were not rooted to the jaw bone but rather within sockets.

TAKING IN THE TRIASSIC
Efraasia

Efraasia had a small head and light body. Its hind limbs were longer than its forelimbs; it is thought that it walked on all fours most of the time but ran on two. It has been recently theorized that most Efraasia fossils excavated so far belonged to juveniles. If so, a mature specimen could have possibly been up to 20 feet long.

Scientific name: Efraasia
Length: 9 feet
Diet: Herbivore (Some omnivore)
Habitat: Dry highlands
Discovered: Europe
Era: Late Triassic

WATCH OUT FOR PAPERCUTZ™

Welcome to the frenzied, fast-paced fourth DINOSAUR EXPLORERS graphic novel by Redcode and Albbie, writers, and Air Team, artists, from Papercutz, those Manosaurs dedicated to publishing great graphic novels for all ages. I'm Jim Salicrup, the Editor-in-Chief and someone who says "Smurftastic" more than anyone else, here to let you know a bit about what's going on behind-the-scenes here at Papercutz...

You've witnessed for yourself, in this very graphic novel, how dangerous life can be for Emily, Rain, Lil S, Sean, Stone, and the rest, millions of years ago back in the Triassic. But do you think things would be any safer in the far-flung future? Or on another world? For twelve-year-old Erik Farrel, who ran away from home and woke up without his memory on a patchwork planet, things are very, very dangerous. Of course, I'm talking about the award-winning Papercutz graphic novel series THE ONLY LIVING BOY, by David Gallaher, writer, and Steve Ellis, artist. Papercutz has recently collected the entire five-volume series in deluxe omnibus editions, available in either paperback or hardcover. Not only do you get all the comics from the five THE ONLY LIVING BOY graphic novels, but two bonus stories as well.

In case you're thinking that you're lucky to be alive now, when there are no longer any dinosaurs around, think again. While they're not necessarily dinosaurs, there are all sorts of strange beasties lurking just below the ocean's surface. You can discover some of the wilder ones in SEA CREATURES #1 and #2, by Christophe Cazenove, writer, and Thierry Jytéry, artist, another great Papercutz graphic novel series, also available wherever books are sold (and in libraies too!). And here's the crazy part—in SEA CREATURES, you get to discover all the facts about these ocean dwellers from the SEA CREATURES themselves! While everything they tell you is based on fact, the creators of the series let the SEA CREATURES speak—to tell you their fascinating tales in their own words.

Oh, here's a real behind-the-scenes Papercutz story that proves what a dinosaur I am! When editing "Trapped in the Triassic," I was confused when on page 150 Emily's dinosaur friend is told, "Hey, Yoshi!" I won't tell you how long I spent poring over the previous 149 pages trying to figure out who Yoshi was! It wasn't until young Papercutz Managing Editor Jeff Whitman informed me that Yoshi was Mario and Luigi's dinosaur sidekick that I finally got the joke! I guess being older than Dr. Da Vinci can have its drawbacks...

So, on that slightly embarrassing note, I'll leave you to explore the future with THE ONLY LIVING BOY, search the present for SEA CREATURES, and return to the past for DINOSAUR EXPLORERS #5 "Lost in the Jurassic," coming soon!

Thanks,

Jim

STAY IN TOUCH!

EMAIL: salicrup@papercutz.com
WEB: papercutz.com
TWITTER: @papercutzgn
INSTAGRAM: @papercutzgn
FACEBOOK: PAPERCUTZGRAPHICNOVELS
FAN MAIL: Papercutz, 160 Broadway, Suite 700, East Wing, New York, NY 10038

TEST YOURSELF!

01 Which geological age did the Triassic belong to?

A - 3rd

B - 5th

C - 7th

02 What geographical phenomenon does the image below refer to?

A - The union of lands and reduction of coastlines

B - The melting of glaciers and an increase of water levels

C - A strong earthquake that sank land under the sea

Ⓐ Hypsognathus

Ⓑ Mastodonsaurus

03 Which one of these is the earliest mammal?

Ⓒ Eozostrodon

04 Which order did this pelvis structure belong to?

A - Saurischia

B - Ornithischia

C - Therapoda

05 Which was the most common species during the early Triassic?

A - Lystrosaurus

B - Mastodonsaurus

C - Placerias

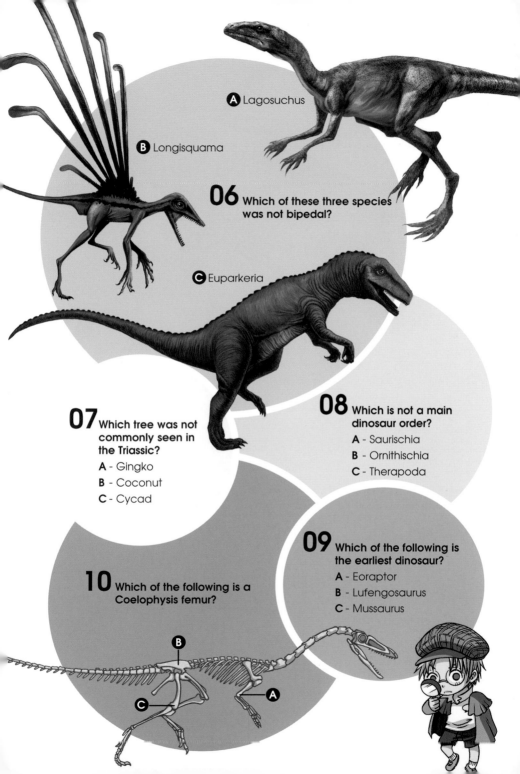

A Lagosuchus

B Longisquama

06 Which of these three species was not bipedal?

C Euparkeria

07 Which tree was not commonly seen in the Triassic?
A - Gingko
B - Coconut
C - Cycad

08 Which is not a main dinosaur order?
A - Saurischia
B - Ornithischia
C - Therapoda

09 Which of the following is the earliest dinosaur?
A - Eoraptor
B - Lufengosaurus
C - Mussaurus

10 Which of the following is a Coelophysis femur?

11 Which is a Staurikosaurus?

A

B

C

12 What is the purpose of a Henodus beak?
A - To chew shells
B - Decoration
C - To show off

13 Where is the Psephoderma's beak?

A

B

C

14 Which tooth belonged to the Plateosaurus?

A   B   C

15 Which group did the Archosauria belong to?
A - Anapsid
B - Synapsid
C - Diapsids

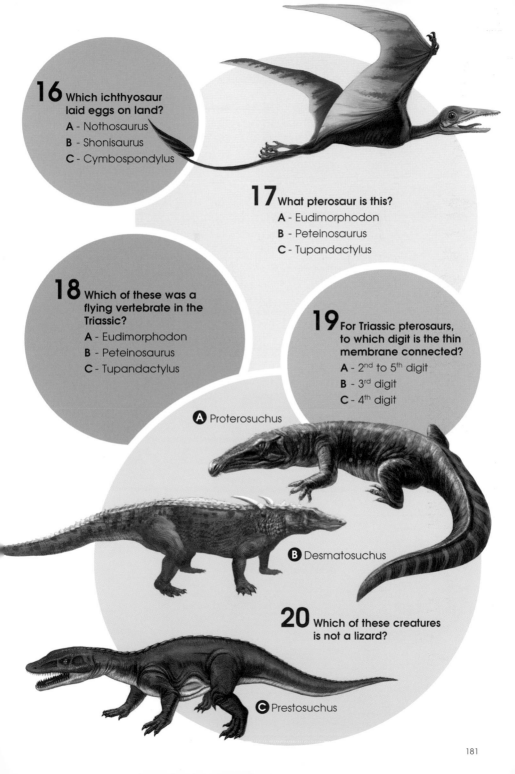

16 Which ichthyosaur laid eggs on land?
A - Nothosaurus
B - Shonisaurus
C - Cymbospondylus

17 What pterosaur is this?
A - Eudimorphodon
B - Peteinosaurus
C - Tupandactylus

18 Which of these was a flying vertebrate in the Triassic?
A - Eudimorphodon
B - Peteinosaurus
C - Tupandactylus

19 For Triassic pterosaurs, to which digit is the thin membrane connected?
A - 2nd to 5th digit
B - 3rd digit
C - 4th digit

A Proterosuchus

B Desmatosuchus

20 Which of these creatures is not a lizard?

C Prestosuchus

ANSWERS

01 C	02 A	03 C	04 B	05 A
06 B	07 B	08 C	09 A	10 C
11 B	12 A	13 B	14 C	15 C
16 A	17 A	18 B	19 C	20 B

All correct?
Congrats! You're as smart as I am! I think.

16 – 19 correct?
I'm actually smarter than the Doctor! Don't tell anyone!

12 -15 correct?
Don't just take in knowledge— apply it to real life!

8-11 correct?
What? You're smarter than me? Impossible!

4 – 7 correct?
Huh, looks like we both can use some work! Let's go to the library! Studying's better with friends!

0-3 correct?
Don't worry, you're as S-M-R-T smart as me!

THE SMURFS #21

THE GARFIELD SHOW #6

BARBIE #1

THE SISTERS #1

TROLLS #1

GERONIMO STILTON #17

THEA STILTON #6

SEA CREATURES #1

DINOSAUR EXPLORERS #1

SCARLETT

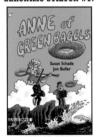
ANNE OF GREEN
BAGELS #1

DRACULA MARRIES
FRANKENSTEIN!

THE RED SHOES

THE LITTLE
MERMAID

FUZZY BASEBALL

HOTEL
TRANSYLVANIA #1

THE LOUD HOUSE #1

MANOSAURS #1

THE ONLY LIVING
BOY #5

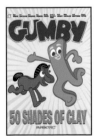
GUMBY #1

MORE GREAT GRAPHIC NOVEL SERIES AVAILABLE FROM

PAPERCUTZ™

papercutz.com

All available where ebooks are sold.

Geological Time Spiral

MESOZOIC ERA

205 million years ago

250 million years ago

Jurassic Period

510 million years ago

Trias Period

570 million years ago

Cambrian Period | Ordovician P

290 million years ago

PALEOZOIC ERA

Permian Period

Carboniferous Period

355 million years ago

PRECAMBRIAN

1 billion years ago

2 billion years ago

4.5 billion years ago

3 billion years ago